DAVID MORTIMORE BAXTER

Jealous!

by Karen Tayleur

illustrated by Brann Garvey

STONE ARCH BOOKS
www.stonearchbooks.com

David Mortimore Baxter is published by Stone Arch Books
151 Good Counsel Drive, P.O. Box 669
Mankato, Minnesota 56002
www.stonearchbooks.com

Library of Congress Cataloging-in-Publication Data
Tayleur, Karen.
    Jealous: On the Sidelines with David Mortimore Baxter / by Karen Tayleur;
illustrated by Brann Garvey.
    p. cm. — (David Mortimore Baxter)
    ISBN 978-1-4342-1198-9 (library binding)
    [1. Jealousy—Fiction. 2. Motion pictures—Production and direction—
Fiction. 3. Friendship—Fiction.] I. Garvey, Brann, ill. II. Title.
PZ7.T21149Je 2009
[Fic]—dc22   2008031674

Summary
Joe, David's best friend, has always dreamed of being in a movie. So why doesn't
David feel happy when Joe is cast in the new movie being filmed in Bays Park?
Everyone in town is thrilled by Hollywood choosing their city for the movie's
location, but David just feels left out. Can he get over his jealousy, or will he risk
losing his best friend?

Creative Director: Heather Kindseth
Graphic Designer: Carla Zetina-Yglesias

Photo Credits
Delaney Photography, cover

1 2 3 4 5 6 14 13 12 11 10 09

Table of Contents

CHAPTER 1

JOE'S SECRET

"I'd like to thank my agent. My producer and director. My co-stars. The crew — all those guys behind the scenes — you all do an amazing job. And, of course, my family. I couldn't have done it without you. **You rock!**"

"What are you doing, **Joe**?" I asked.

Joe was standing in front of my hallway mirror, holding onto a soda bottle like it was a microphone. He had the kind of 𝔾𝕆𝕆𝔽𝕐 grin he gets when he's been caught doing something *weird*.

"Hey, David," he said.

"So?" I asked. "What are you doing?"

Joe hid the bottle behind his back. "I was just waiting for you," he said. "What took you so long, anyway?"

Joe and I were going to visit **Bec**. She wanted to tell us something, but **she wouldn't talk about it on the phone** when she called that morning.

"David, I need to call a Secret Club meeting," she had whispered **dramatically**.

"Why are you whispering?" I asked her.

"I found out some really INTERESTING information. I think one of our Secret Club members will find it very interesting, anyway," she said.

"Me?" I asked.

"Just come to my house," she said.

There were only three members of the Secret Club. Joe, Bec, and me. The honorary members were **Boris**, my dog, and Ralph, Bec's pet rat. The Secret Club had rules and special handshakes and secret signals, but the signals were always changing because we kept forgetting what they were. Our current secret signal was a cat meow. We usually used birdcalls, but **Joe kept mixing them up.**

The walk to Bec's apartment took a while, because Joe kept trying to avoid the CRACKS in the pavement.

I was busy telling him how much money
I'd saved for the bike I wanted to buy.
Then I stopped.

"What are you doing, Joe?" I asked as I watched
him leap sideways.

"It's an old **show business** thing," he explained.
"It's bad luck to stand on the cracks."

"Show business?" I asked.

"Did I say show business?" asked Joe. He jumped
to avoid an **enormous** crack that went through the
sidewalk in front of us.

There's something you should know about **Joe**. His
parents own a video store, and he spends a
lot of time watching movies. Sometimes he
comes to school dressed as a **pirate** or a
SECRET AGENT or an **astronaut**. Ms. Stacey,
our teacher, doesn't mind because, except for the
costumes, Joe is a trouble-free student. Her words, not
mine. Anyway, I was starting to think that whatever
movie Joe had last watched was making him act a
little WEIRD.

"What movie did you watch last night, Joe?"
I asked.

"No time for movies," said Joe. "I'm busy with
other things."

We finally made it to Bec's apartment building, so I
didn't bother to ask what other things Joe
was doing. Joe pushed Bec's intercom button
and WOOFed into it.

Bec's voice came out of the speaker. "Hello, Joe.
You're supposed to *meow*, not WOOF," she said. The
door clicked open.

"How did she know it was me?" asked **Joe**.

"Good guess," I said.

Bec met us inside. "Let's go to the laundry room,"
she said. "Mom's cleaning the apartment."

The laundry room was down in the
basement of her building. It was a
great place to have Secret Club meetings.
It was warm and sticky in a nice way. There was
usually a washing machine making noise, so **no one
could listen to our conversations.**

We sat down in a corner of the laundry room, with our backs to the wall. That way, we could keep an eye on people coming in. Two dryers whirred away near the door.

"What's going on, Bec?" I asked.

Bec pulled a piece of paper from her jacket pocket and carefully unfolded it.

"Mom got this from a friend of a friend of hers," she said. "It's top secret for now."

The flyer read:

To the residents of Bays Park

Considering a new career? The producers of Two Stone County *are searching for extras for this new film, which explores our pioneer days.*

There will be two open audition days. We invite professional actors and amateurs alike to come along and join in the fun.

Then the paper had times and dates and where to go.

"This is it, Joe," said Bec. "This is the chance you've been waiting for."

Joe wanted to be an actor when he grew up. It's all he ever talked about when people asked him what he wanted to do with his life. When I say people, I mean mostly adults.

I was surprised. For a guy who had just gotten the **chance of a lifetime**, Joe was acting as if it was **no big deal.**

Just then, a little kid came into the laundry room. Bec shoved the paper back in her pocket, and I started talking about a homework project.

The kid stopped one of the dryers and felt the clothes inside. They must have still been wet, because he grunted, quickly shut the dryer door, and turned it on again. **Then he walked out without even looking at us.**

Bec pulled the paper out again. "So, Joe, what do you think?" she asked. **"Isn't this cool?** Are you going to try out?"

Joe was spinning his soda bottle around on the floor. "I don't think so," he said.

"What? Are you **crazy**?" I asked. "Look, I know auditions are *scary*. But we can help you. Bec and me and even Zoe if you want." **Zoe** was  my older sister. She made costumes for the local theater company, so she probably knew all about auditions.

"That's okay," said Joe. "Thanks anyway, but **I'm not going** to the auditions."

"Joe," said **Bec**. She had that look on her face that means that she's going to go on and on about something, and we were going to have to sit there and wait until she'd finished talking. Before she could start her speech, Joe stopped spinning his bottle. He stood up and dusted himself off.

"I'm not going to the audition," he said, **"and that's final."**

"That's it?" I asked.

"Yep," he said. He headed for the laundry room door.

"You're **definitely** not going for an audition?" asked Bec.

"That's right," said Joe as he reached the door. Then he turned around and added, "I don't need to. I'm already in the movie."

CHAPTER 2

OLD SALAMI

That was why Joe had been acting so strange. **He'd been keeping a secret from me.** A really big secret, which is something Joe usually can't do.

Getting a part in a movie was the biggest thing that ever happened in Joe's life, and he hadn't even told me. He hadn't asked for my advice or called me as soon as he knew.

That made me feel weird inside, like I'd **eaten old salami.** Why had Joe kept the secret from us?

"Get back here right now and **tell us everything,**" **Bec** demanded.

I didn't say anything. I looked at **Joe**. He couldn't even look me in the eye.

Joe sat back down between Bec and me. **"It's a long story,"** he said.

Bec just tapped her foot. I kept staring at Joe, who still wouldn't look at me.

"A woman came into my parents' video store two days ago," Joe said finally. "I was behind the counter and she came up and asked me to be in the new movie."

"That's not a long story," I said.

Bec pushed me. "So who was she?" Bec asked. "What did she say? Come on, Joe, **spill it**."

"I don't know," **Joe** said. "She said she was in charge of getting actors for the movie. She asked if I'd done any acting before, so I said I had a lot of experience playing different roles."

Bec and I looked at each other. "Dressing up in your costumes **doesn't count**," Bec said.

"I never said I'd acted in anything," said Joe. "I just said I played lots of roles."

He had a point there.

"But why didn't you tell us?" said Bec. "This is so exciting. I know someone who is going to be in a movie. **How cool!**"

"Yeah, why didn't you tell us, Joe?" I echoed.

"It was SECRET," said Joe. "She made me promise not to tell anyone until she sent the flyers out."

"But Joe, we're your best friends," said **Bec**. I nodded.

"I know," said Joe, looking down. "But a promise is a promise. And this is really important to me."

Joe looked me in the eye. I didn't know what to say.

"It's okay," Bec said finally. "We understand. But the flyers are out now. So you can talk about it, right?"

"I guess so," said Joe.

"So what part did you get?" asked Bec.

"She didn't tell me," said Joe, "and I forgot to ask her."

We spent the next half hour talking about the movie and how cool it was that Joe was going to be in it. And even though I said nice things and kept a smile on my face, deep down **the bad salami feeling didn't go away.**

The next day was Monday, which is my **least favorite day**. Monday meant getting up early for school, eating breakfast in a hurry, and making sure I had my homework in my backpack.

Of course, it's very hard to get all these things done. Sometimes I miss breakfast. **Sometimes I sleep in.** But usually I leave my homework at home and **get into trouble** from our teacher, Ms. Stacey. Today was no different.

"Please pass your homework to the front of the class," said **Ms. Stacey** after she took attendance.

I slapped my forehead. I'd left my homework sitting on the hallway table near my front door at home. I'd been too busy thinking about how cool it would be to ride the new bike I wanted to school. I'd forgotten to pick my homework up.

Luckily, I have a whole list of excuses that I use for emergencies like this.

Unluckily, Ms. Stacey didn't give me a chance to use one.

"And if your name is David Mortimore Baxter," Ms. Stacey said, "and you do not have your homework, feel free to stay behind at recess and clean out the recycling bin."

Rose Thornton (**my biggest enemy**) and her friends laughed. I looked at Joe for some support, but he was busy staring out the window like he hadn't heard a thing.

Then Rose raised her hand. She looked around at the class with a look that said she knew something we didn't know. Then she coughed a couple of times, just to get Ms. Stacey's attention.

Finally, Ms. Stacey looked up and sighed. "Yes, Rose?" she said.

"I have a **special announcement** to make," said Rose. She was practically standing on her chair.

Ms. Stacey sighed again. "Go ahead, Rose," she said.

Rose walked up to the front of the room. Then she waited for everyone to be QUIET before she began talking.

"As you know," she said, "my mother has a very *important* job and knows a lot of very *important* people."

A few kids nodded. We all knew that. Rose never stopped talking about how **important** her mom's job was. Mrs. Thornton worked at a public relations company. No one really knew what that was, but Rose made sure we knew it was **important**.

"Well, in her line of business, she gets a lot of *important* information," said Rose. "A lot."

She waited a moment to let this news seep into our brains. **No one said anything.**

"Anyway," said Rose. "I have some information that my mother has agreed to let me pass onto you before anyone else in Bays Park. It is still a SECRET, but—"

"Please hurry up, Rose," said **Ms. Stacey**.

"Okay," Rose said. "A movie is going to be made in Bays Park and the company is looking for extras. That means other actors," she explained, **as if we were all dumb.**

Ms. Stacey nodded and said, "Yes, I have a flyer here about that. I was going to hand it out at the end of the day."

Rose seemed to SHRINK a little. "Oh," she said. "Well, I just wanted you all to know just in case you were interested in trying out. Of course, I'll be trying out. I *have a private audition*, because of my mother's contacts."

"I didn't even know she needed glasses," I whispered to Joe. My joke was lost in the noise as Rose's friends burst into excited clapping.

I watched Rose's cheeks turn pink with pleasure. That's what I didn't like about Rose. She'd been pretending to help us all out by giving us some inside information, but really, she just wanted to show off that  she had a private audition. **She was just rubbing our faces in it.**

"That's nothing," I said loudly as the clapping died down. **"Joe already has a part in the movie!"**

"What?" screeched Rose. Her cheeks turned from light pink to red.

The class erupted into a babble of noise. Some kids came up to slap **Joe** on the back. Everyone was talking and yelling.

"Okay, **settle down,**" said Ms. Stacey. "That's enough for now."

But when I looked at **Rose Thornton's** face, I knew that wasn't the end of it.

Not even close.

CHAPTER 3

During recess, **I had to clean the recycling bin.**
But Bec told me later that kids from all over school
had talked to Joe during recess. Most of them just
wanted to see the kid who was going to be in a movie,
but some came to get his advice on how they could
get a job as an extra.

Even **Victor Sneddon,** the school bully (and
Rose's cousin), gave Joe a slap on the back.
That's as friendly as Victor gets.

The thing is, **Joe can be pretty shy sometimes,**
even though he likes acting. Bec helped him out with
all the attention until the bell rang.

Later that night, Bec called me. "Seriously, David,
I think Joe is going to need our ℍ𝔼𝕃ℙ," she said.

"Hmm," I said. I still hadn't lost that **bad feeling**
in my stomach, but I knew she was right. The only
way Joe was going to get through this whole acting
job was if Bec and I helped him.

"Leave it to me," I said. **Taking charge** of the whole situation made me feel better.

Then I went to see my sister, Zoe. Sometimes she has really good ideas, although I'd NEVER tell her that.

I knocked on her bedroom door. I knew she was in there, but you would never want to open her bedroom door without knocking.  **She would just go crazy.** Then she'd tell my mom, who always takes Zoe's side.

There was no answer, so I knocked again.

"What?" **Zoe yelled**.

"Can I come in?" I asked. "It's me, David."

The door opened. "I know who it is, **Dribbles**," she said with a frown. Dribbles is her nickname for me. It has been since I was really little. I don't really want to talk about why she calls me that. "What do you want?" she asked.

"I want your advice," I said.

Zoe *scowled*, but she let me in. "Don't touch anything," she warned. "And **don't look at my laptop!**"

It was hard to see anything inside Zoe's room. The curtains were closed, and it was like being **inside a cave.** Her laptop was open. The latest copy of *Stars Weekly* was on her bed.

"Okay, what's up?" asked Zoe.

I told her all about Joe's chance at **superstardom.**

"Superstar?" Zoe asked. She laughed. "Maybe he should take it one step at a time."

"You read all about Hollywood," I said, pointing to the magazine on her bed. "You must know how it works. What should Joe be doing to make sure he gets 𝔽𝔸𝕄𝕆𝕌𝕊?"

"There are some things he should be doing right now," said Zoe. She sat down at her laptop, made a list, and printed it out.

Joe the superstar — things to consider

- **Agent** — This person helps to get you into auditions and get the best out of your contract.

- **Agent fee** — This should be about 20%, but it could be higher.

- **Fee for job** — Decide how much you are going to ask for, then ask for more.

- **Head shots** — Should have photographs for auditions.

- **Resume for auditions**

- **Makeup artist** — All superstars have their own makeup artists.

- **Hair stylist** — See above.

- **Lifestyle coach** — To help keep you on track once you are a superstar.

- **Singing lessons** — Joe may need help with this.

- **Dancing lessons** — See above.

- **Drama coach** — For acting lessons.

- **Secretary** — To answer fan mail.

- **Personal chef** — To cook food.

- **Financial adviser** — To make sure you don't spend all your money.

I read through the list once. Then I read it again.

"Thanks, Zoe," I said, "but **I don't even know what some of these things are.**" I read the list again. "Lifestyle coach? What's a lifestyle coach?" I asked. "And hair stylist? Joe handles his hair **just fine** right now."

"You asked for my help," Zoe said. "So I'm giving it to you." She picked up *Star Weekly*. "How do you think these people got to where they are? **Talent**? Taking classes?" She shook her head. "It's all about your people. If you don't have people looking out for you, you're not going anywhere. *Do you get it?*"

I didn't really, but I nodded anyway.

"Okay. Then **be a good friend** and give this to Joe," Zoe said. She shoved the list in my face.

"Good luck," she said. Then her cell phone rang, so she pushed me out and shut the door in my face.

I stood in the hallway and read through the list again. I always thought being a superstar was the **easiest job on earth**. I didn't know there was so much to do.

I folded the paper and shoved it in my pocket.

"**I am a good friend,**" I said to **Boris**, who happened to be sleeping in the hallway.

He just lifted an eyelid.

Then I added, "**And if Joe is going to be a superstar, he is going to need all the friends he can get.**"

CHAPTER 4

NOT A REGULAR KID

I took Zoe's list to school the next day. When I found Joe, I showed him the list.

He laughed nervously. "I'm not a superstar, David," he said. **"I'm just a regular kid."**

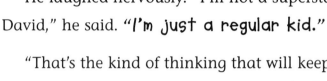

"That's the kind of thinking that will keep you just a regular kid, Joe," I said. "You have to **believe in yourself**. There are plenty of people who are going to want to see you **fail** at this."

"There are?" Joe asked.

"You just have to give it your best shot," I said. **"Bec and I are right behind you.** You know that, don't you?"

Joe nodded.

Elly Van Veen, **our class bookworm**, walked by. She gave Joe a huge smile. "Hi, Joe," she said.

"Hello," mumbled Joe.

"You need to look at this list," I said. "Take it home and STUDY it. When do you go on set?"

"Huh?" asked Joe.

Chris Lang walked past, bouncing a basketball. "Hey, champ," he said to Joe.

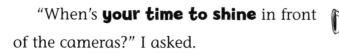

"Hi," said Joe.

"When's **your time to shine** in front of the cameras?" I asked.

"Oh. I'm not sure. I think it's a couple of weeks," said Joe.

"That's not a lot of time," I said. **"We have a lot of work to do."**

"We do?" Joe asked.

Lee Hall ran past us, and then stopped. He turned around and smiled at Joe. "Hey, Joe," Lee said.

"Hi, Lee," said Joe.

"It's okay, Joe," I said. "With Bec and me guiding you, you're going to be huge. Now show me that **million-dollar smile."**

Joe gave me a weird smile. **It made him look like he was in pain.**

"Yeah, we're going to have to work on that," I said.

* * *

In class, someone had drawn a **huge yellow star** on the board and written the words "Joe Pagnopolous" underneath it.

Joe's face turned red when he saw that, but I told him he was just going to have to get used to it. **He was a star now.**

Joe's face wasn't the only one that was red.

Rose Thornton looked like she wanted to hit someone. **Probably me.** I guess she wished that she were the one who already had a part in the movie.

I kind of felt *sorry* for Rose, so I walked over to her desk to cheer her up.

"So, how's your private audition going, Rose?" I asked.

Rose looked up at the ceiling. Then she turned to one of her friends.

"Katerina, can you hear anything?" Rose asked.

Katerina looked at me. Then she looked at Rose. "Um, yes," said Katerina.

"I think it must be the air conditioning," said Rose.

That meant Rose was IGNORING me, which was fine with me. I decided to talk to Katerina instead.

"Are you going to try out for the movie, Kat?" I asked.

"Katerina, I can still hear that noise," interrupted Rose. "It's really starting to ANNOY me."

Katerina just shrugged at me.

"Kat," I said, "please tell Rose that she shouldn't be too jealous that Joe is starring in the movie. I am sure they will be able to find a small part for her."

Rose's face got redder. She said, "Katerina, please tell that air-conditioning noise that if it doesn't be quiet I will shut it off for good."

I was just thinking of a really good reply when Ms. Stacey came in and class was starting. I had to go back to my seat.

That is, I tried to go back to my seat. Louis Debono was sitting next to Joe, where I usually sit.

"I think you're sitting in my seat, Louis," I said.

"So sit in another one," said Louis.

"But **it's my seat**," I insisted.

Louis pretended to look all over the seat. **"Don't see your name on it,"** he said.

As long as I can remember, Joe and I have been sitting next to each other. That's just the way it is.

"Joe, don't you want me to sit next to you?" I asked.

Joe looked **embarrassed**. "Well, David does usually sit there," he said quietly.

"Find a seat, please, David," said **Ms. Stacey**. "We can't wait all day."

I sat in the front of the class next to James Goh. James is all right. He's **obsessed** with wrestling, so we talked about that for a while.

Then Ms. Stacey gave us a spelling test and I forgot all about the movie for the next fifteen minutes.

And even though I hate spelling tests, **those were the happiest fifteen minutes of my day.**

CHAPTER 5

DIFFERENT

Once people found out that Joe was going to be in the movie, **everyone** wanted to be friends with him.

At recess, Joe and Bec and I usually hang out under the oak tree. Nobody else hangs out there. But that day, **half the school** seemed to be hanging out under the **oak tree**.

Most kids just wanted to talk to Joe, but some wanted his AUTOGRAPH. Others just hung around on the edges pretending they just happened to be there.

And it wasn't just the kids who wanted to be friends with Joe.

Mr. Edwards, the school janitor, asked if Joe could set up a meeting with Harrison Ford. Mr. Edwards was Harrison Ford's **number-one fan** in Bays Park. He was president of the fan club and everything.

"I don't even know if Harrison Ford is in the movie," said Joe.

Mr. Edwards just nodded and winked. "Sure you don't, Joe," he said. Then he walked away, chuckling.

During gym class, **Mr. Mildendew**, our gym teacher, made Joe run **an extra lap**.

He said it was because Joe took a **shortcut** during the second lap of our run, but we all knew it was because Joe had **refused** to try to find out if Julia Roberts was in the movie.

"I don't think they'd tell me, Mr. Mildendew," said Joe.

Mr. Mildendew agreed. "You're right, Joe," he said. "They probably wouldn't." Then he made Joe run the extra lap. When I said **that wasn't fair**, he made me run with Joe.

I didn't mind too much. **I like running.** But I could see that **Rose Thornton** had a smirk on her face. It made me want to say something really mean, except I couldn't think of anything. So I just started running with Joe.

"Let's just see Rose 𝕊𝕄𝕀𝕃𝔼 when she doesn't get a part in the movie," I said to Joe as we ran.

"I wish I'd never gotten the stupid part in the stupid movie," said Joe.

"What?" I asked. "Why? **What's gotten into you, Joe?**"

"What's gotten into me?" Joe repeated. "What's gotten into everyone else, is more like it. **Everyone has gone nuts.** My teachers are acting strange. And even my parents are walking around like I just won an Academy Award or something. Every time I sneeze, Mom wants to take my temperature in case I'm coming down with a cold. And every time I talk to Dad, he keeps interrupting me to tell me to speak more clearly."

"That would be ANNOYING," I agreed.

"Everyone is treating me different," Joe said. "Like I'm not me anymore."

"But this is what you wanted," I said. "To be an actor. This is really cool, Joe. **Aren't you happy?**"

"Sure," Joe said slowly. "I'm happy. I just wish everything else was the **same**."

"Why don't you come over this weekend," I said.

I thought about it. Then I added, "We can hang out with Bec, maybe brush up on our S P Y I N G. We haven't done that for a while."

Spying was one of the things that the members of the **Secret Club** did.

We mostly spied on each other, but sometimes we spied on other people, like my neighbor, **Mr. McCafferty**. Or my sister, Zoe.

Joe smiled. "I'd like that," he said.

"Okay," I said. **"Good."**

* * *

When I told Mom that night that Joe and Bec might come for lunch on Sunday, she said that she hoped Joe would be HAPPY to have lasagna.

"Why wouldn't he be?" I asked. "We always have lasagna on Sunday."

"That's not true, David," said Mom. "Sometimes we have a roast. Maybe I should cook a roast. Joe always has **second helpings** when I cook my famous pot roast."

"Lasagna's fine, Mom. **Joe won't care**," I said.

But Mom wasn't listening. She started talking about dessert.

I went to my room. There was a scratching sound at the door. I opened it and let **Boris** in.

"Hi, pal," I said. "At least you haven't started acting WEIRD."

Boris flopped down on my foot. I gave him a pat and a scratch behind the ears.

"Hey, maybe you could get a part in the movie," I said.

Boris began to scratch himself with his back paw. I added, "They can't make a movie about pioneers without a dog."

Boris just yawned and kept scratching.

"Maybe I could teach you some TRICKS," I said. "Then we could go see that lady who gave Joe the part in the movie."

I spent the next hour trying to teach Boris some basic dog tricks.

I couldn't believe I hadn't tried to teach him any tricks before. But after an hour of training, **I began to understand why.**

The closest Boris got to carrying out a command was lying down. And he'd already been lying down when I told him to lie down, so I don't know if that counts.

I decided that Boris was never going to be **a famous dog actor.**

"You're just going to have to be plain old Boris Baxter, house pet," I told Boris. He stopped scratching long enough to **slobber** on my hand.

"I'm going to have to focus on helping Joe," I said.

I couldn't wait for the weekend. **Joe wouldn't know what hit him.**

CHAPTER 6

OPERATION SUPERSTAR

Saturday was **Operation Superstar.** I talked to Bec about it. We both agreed that if Joe wanted to be a movie star, he would need our help.

"We can't meet at my place," said Bec. "Mom is cleaning."

"Okay, my place it is," I said.

We met at my house right after breakfast on Saturday morning. The **first** thing we talked about was whether Joe needed an agent or not.

"My dad said that he would be my agent," said Joe. "And he'd only charge me fifteen percent. Whatever that means."

"I think maybe your father was JOKING," said Bec, rolling her eyes.

Joe just shrugged.

I crossed **agent** and **agent fee** off the list.

"Have you discussed your pay yet with the producers?" I asked Joe.

"I haven't even met the producers," said Joe. "Besides, I'd do it for free."

"That's why Bec and I are here to help you," I said. "You'd do it for free? Do you think that Will Smith works for free?"

Joe shook his head.

"Of course he doesn't," I said. "Do you think he has that **huge** mansion and COOL cars and a **private** jet—"

"I don't think he has a private jet," interrupted Bec.

"Whatever," I said. "Anyway, do you think he got all that by **acting for free**? These producer guys, they're in it for the money. This is not a charity. They don't let us in for free at the movie theater, do they?"

Joe shook his head.

"That's right," I said. "**This is business.** Now, there's got to be a list of fees for actors somewhere. I'll look into it for you. What's next on our list, Bec?"

"Photographs," she said. "I brought my camera with me."

"Well, before you take any photos, maybe we should look at the rest of **the list**," I said.

That's when I went to get Zoe.

"You want me to do Joe's makeup and hair?" **Zoe** said. "But I've only ever done that for theater performers."

"Same thing," I said. "Come on, Zoe. Joe needs your help."

Zoe sighed. "Fine," she said.

Joe wasn't too EXCITED about Zoe doing his face and hair, but as Bec pointed out, he'd have to put up with it if he was going to be in movies. All actors wore **makeup**. Even Johnny Depp, Joe's favorite actor.

"Especially Johnny Depp," said Zoe. Then she got to work on Joe.

When Zoe was done, Joe certainly did look different. She'd put some **stuff in his hair**. The stuff made his hair stand up.

Then she put some **dark stuff under his eyes** and **pink stuff on his cheeks** that made him look kind of 𝔼𝕍𝕀𝕃.

"What do you think?" Zoe asked.

"Fantastic," said **Bec**. She grabbed her camera and started taking pictures of Joe. But after a few, she stopped.

"The light in here is *all wrong*," she said. "We're going to have to go outside."

Joe shook his head. "I am not going outside," he said. "What if someone sees me?"

We made Joe go outside. Then we looked around for a good background.

"How about a **tree**?" said Bec.

I shook my head.

"The *house*?" said Zoe.

I shook my head again.

"We need to find something perfect," I said. "Something that says, '*This is who Joe is. Deal with it.*'"

Then I had a great idea. "Stay here," I said. I rushed into the garage and found what I was looking for — a white spray can of paint that we had used at Christmas to make **fake snow** on our windows. The paint was easily removed with water once we'd finished with it.

Back outside, I began painting a message on the brick wall by the driveway.

When I finished my message, I stood back and read it aloud. "**Joe Rules**," it said.

"Stand in front of that, Joe," I said.

"Can we get something to eat?" asked Joe.

"Not until we finish the photo shoot," I said.

It took us about an hour to finish Joe's photos. It wasn't as easy as we thought.

It took **FOREVER** to get Joe in just the right position. Then it took forever for him to loosen up so he didn't look like **a wooden puppet.**

Then the sun went behind a cloud, so we had to wait for it to come out again.

When Bec said we were finally finished, Joe was **exhausted**. "Food," he moaned.

Inside, Mom had just finished making an Operation Superstar lunch.

There were huge turkey sandwiches, chocolate milkshakes, and some **strange-looking** cookies that were fresh from the oven.

"What kind of cookies are those?" I asked, pointing to the cookies.

"I call them my not-quite-right cookies," said Mom, smiling.

Whatever she called them, they tasted great.

"Maybe you could be Joe's private chef when he's famous," I told Mom.

"I'll cross that off our list," said Bec.

After we ate, Joe played outside with Boris while Bec and I looked at the list. We weren't really sure what some of the different people were supposed to do, so we had to use the computer to look it up. We worked on the list for **a couple of hours.**

There were still things left on the list that we hadn't gotten to, but Joe was outside trying to play one-on-one **basketball with Boris.**

"Let's take a break," I told Bec.

Bec agreed. We spent the rest of the afternoon playing basketball. Then Dad came home and saw my spray paint on the brick wall.

"David Mortimore Baxter!" he yelled.

Then Bec and Joe decided it was time to go home. We agreed that the day had been a SUCCESS. We were going to do some spying the next day, and they were both coming over for lunch.

That night, I went to bed feeling pretty pleased with myself. I didn't know then that Operation Superstar would turn out to be **a total waste of time.**

CHAPTER 7

MARLEY GRACE

Marley Grace was the name of the woman who had **discovered** Joe in his parent's video store. I know her name because she called me the day after **Operation Superstar.**

"Hello. Is this David Baxter?" she asked.

Then she'd introduced herself. She said she worked for *Two Stone County*, the movie being filmed in Bays Park.

I started to get ⑂✗⦿ⒾⓉⒺⒹ. I thought maybe she'd heard about my dog, Boris. Maybe she wanted to give him an **audition**!

"How can I help you?" I asked politely. I wanted to show her that I had **good manners**, which I would probably need if I wanted to be a Hollywood pet trainer.

"Well, David, it's more about how I can help you," she said.

I liked the sound of that. "Okay," I said.

She told me that she had just visited Joe at the video store. Joe had shown her Zoe's **superstar list.**

"Oh," I said. I started to feel a little bit STRANGE about that.

"I think you've done a great job with that list," she said.

"Great!" I said.

"But we have it all covered," Marley told me. "Joe's part of the *Two Stone County* team now, so we will be giving him all the help he needs to make this **a wonderful experience.** So you're off the hook. You just leave all the work to us."

"I see," I said.

"Joe wanted me to call and clear that up with you," she said. "But I knew we wouldn't have a problem."

"No problem here," I said.

"Great," Marley said. "Hey, will you be auditioning for *Two Stone County*, David?"

"I don't think so," I said.

I had the **weird salami feeling** in my stomach again. I just wanted to get off the phone.

"Well, if you change your mind, you make sure to come and say hi. I'll be the one rushing around with the clipboard," she said.

"Okay," I said.

But she'd already hung up.

CHAPTER 8

A JERK AT LUNCH

Sunday lunch at my place was kind of an open house. That meant that **anyone who was feeling hungry** could come over and eat something. My mom always cooked enough food for fifty people, even when she was only feeding five.

Gran always comes to Sunday lunch. Gran is my dad's mother. She is **the oldest person I know.** I think she's almost 100 or something. She doesn't hear as well as she used to.

Zoe is her favorite grandchild, and Harry's the youngest, so Gran never picks on him. When Gran comes around, **I try to stay out of her way.**

"Gran's here," said **Mom** when a car honked in the driveway. "Help her with her things, please, David."

Gran walks around with a walking stick, but she never actually uses it to walk with. I have, however, seen her use it as a WEAPON.

"Why can't Harry do it?" I grumbled.

Mom ignored me. "Thank you, David," she said.

When I went outside, Gran *frowned* at me. "What took you so long?" she growled.

"Nice to see you, too, Gran," I muttered. I grabbed a huge box from the back seat of her car.

"Be CAREFUL with that," said Gran.

Then she followed me inside, saying, "Be careful! Put your hand under the bottom of the box. Don't treat it like **a sack of potatoes**, young man. Be gentle with it."

"What's in here, Gran?" I finally asked as I lugged the box inside.

"**You mind your own beeswax,**" she said. That was her way of saying she wasn't going to tell me.

Mom had decided to make lasagna. The smell of it cooking had spread through the house.

Joe and Bec arrived together, and Joe wasn't looking me in the eye again, probably because of Miss Talent Scout's phone call that morning.

"Something smells good," said **Bec**.

"Lasagna," I said.

"Mmmm. My FAVORITE," said **Joe**.

"Well, whatever makes you happy, Joe," I said.

I don't know why I said that. I liked lasagna as much as Joe did.

I didn't have a chance before lunch to talk about the talent scout's call, so I just felt MAD about it.

Gran was in a good mood while we ate. She talked and talked and talked.

I found out what was in the box I'd carried in. It was full of **old clothes** that she was going to give to the movie people.

It was Gran's job as head of the Bays Park Historical Society to hand the box over **personally**. She had to give it to the people who were working on *Two Stone County*.

"I thought Joe might be interested in seeing the costumes before I hand them over to the movie people," Gran explained.

"I'm saving up to get a new bike," I said loudly, out of nowhere. "It has five gears and **a gold-speckled padded seat.**"

"That's nice, dear," said Mom.

Gran was very interested to hear what Joe had to say about the movie. She kept asking him questions, even though **he didn't know very much.**

The more she talked to him, the worse I felt. When she asked him how he got the part in the movie, I interrupted.

"I can tell you that, Gran," I said. "Joe was **discovered** by a person named Marley Grace. She called me this morning, actually. To talk about Joe, **her favorite person in the movie.**"

I looked at Joe. He was busy cutting his lasagna up into little pieces. "But you already knew that, didn't you, Joe?" I asked.

Joe quickly nodded.

Bec kicked me under the table. **"What's your problem, David?"** she whispered.

"Problem?" I said loudly. "**No problem here.**
I just got a call this morning from Marley Grace. She
said Joe doesn't need our help anymore, now that he's
a big star and all. He doesn't care about his friends.
He's too important for his friends. So, there you
go. Can I have another piece of lasagna, Mom?"

"Dribbles," hissed Zoe.

"What?" I said. **I knew I was being a jerk, but I
couldn't stop myself.**

"It's okay," I went on. "I mean, I get it. It's just
that we wasted a whole day yesterday on Operation
Superstar, when we could have been doing something
else. Like **watching paint dry** or something."

"That's enough, David," said Dad.

"David, I'm sorry about the list," Joe began.

"Hey, no problem," I said. "I mean, you're a star
now. You need to **move on** from your old friends.
You'll make new friends now."

"You may leave the table, David," said Mom. Her
voice sounded calm, but really meant she was 𝕄𝔸𝔻.

"But, Mom, I was just saying . . ." I began.

"Now," she said.

Everyone was looking at me. Everyone but Joe, that is, who was staring at his plate as if it were a crystal ball.

I scraped my chair back from the table and thumped out of the room.

I wondered how I could be such a JERK.

I wished I could take it all back.

CHAPTER 9

WHY I FEEL BAD

I stayed in my room for the rest of the afternoon. No one bothered to come and see me, **not** **even Boris.**

After everyone left, **Dad** came in and gave me one of his talks about respect and friendship. Boy, I hate that kind of talk.

Later that night I tried to call Joe to apologize. His mom said he was too busy to come to the phone. He was **steaming his vocal cords**, or something.

"You understand, don't you, David?" Joe's mom asked.

I wondered if Joe had told her about lunch. She seemed friendly, so he probably hadn't.

"Sure," I said.

I hung up the phone. Then I went to Zoe's room.

The sign on Zoe's door said, "Studying in progress." That meant:

STUDYING
IN
PROGRESS

a) she was **instant messaging** her friends on her laptop

b) she was **texting** her friends on her cell phone

c) she was **talking** to her friends on her cell phone

d) she was actually **studying.**

I walked down the hall to the computer room. The door was open. I could see Dad at the computer with a pile of papers.

I kept going. I could hear the TV on in the living room. It sounded like one of Mom's shows where everybody marries everyone else and people are dying and people are having babies all over the place. **I didn't want to bother her.**

There was only one person left I could talk to. My brother, Harry.

Normally I don't go into Harry's room. His room is really messy, and it has **a strange smell** — it's a sour, moldy smell that might be from his **gym shoes,** or it might be from whatever **food** is lying at the bottom of his backpack.

Anyway, I took a **deep breath** and went into Harry's room. I didn't knock because I never knock on Harry's door. I don't have to, because **I'm older than he is.**

The smell inside Harry's room wasn't too bad for once, but I couldn't see Harry anywhere. I was just about to leave when I heard a ᑕᐤᑌᏩᕼ from the pile of blankets on the floor.

"Harry?" I said.

The blankets on the floor moved and up popped Harry, like **a creature rising out of a swamp.**

"Hi, David," he said.

Harry told me he was hiding from Mom. I didn't bother telling him that Mom was watching TV, not looking for him.

"So," I said. I sat down on the edge of Harry's bed. I could only sit on the edge because it was **covered** with toys and clothes.

"When are you going to buy your bike?" Harry asked.

"Maybe tomorrow," I said.

Once I'd said it, it sounded like a really good idea. I'd been planning to wait until my birthday so I could ask for some EXTRAS like special brakes, but that could wait.

"So," I repeated.

"What's wrong, David?" asked Harry.

"Wrong? Nothing's wrong," I said. I shifted back onto the bed a little. **A pile of dirty clothes** hit the floor.

"Are you still in trouble with Mom and Dad?" Harry asked.

I didn't bother to answer that.

"Did **Dad** talk to you?" he asked.

I nodded.

"Oh," said Harry.

"So what do your friends think about *Two Stone County*?" I asked finally.

"What about it?" Harry asked.

"About the whole thing," I said. "Are any of them going to audition?"

"No," said **Harry**. "It's not like it's *The Amazing Ten*. If it was *The Amazing Ten*, I'd be lining up now for an audition."

"But, Harry, *The Amazing Ten* is a cartoon. You couldn't act in a cartoon," I said. Sometimes I wondered about my brother.

"Well, *Two Stone County* sounds boring," Harry said. "It's just some story about the olden days," he added. "Who cares about that?"

"Joe's going to be in it," I said.

"I know," Harry said. "Do you think he could introduce me to Tractor Man from *The Amazing Ten*?"

I just shook my head. When I left the room, Harry hid under the blankets again.

I wanted to call **Bec**, but I wasn't sure she was still talking to me. **I felt really bad.** Not just about the whole lunchtime thing.

I went to my room and tried to write it out.

Dad always says that writing out your troubles can take them **out of your head and into the world.** Once your trouble is written down, it becomes real. Then it's easier to deal with.

Why I feel bad

Because I'm not in the movie? (No, that is not the problem. I don't even want to be in the movie. For real.)

Because Joe is in the movie? (No. I'm happy that Joe is going to be in it.)

Because Boris is not in the movie? (Maybe, but I don't think so.)

Because Rose Thornton is annoying? (True, but she's always annoying.)

Because I was mean to Joe? (Yep, but I already felt bad before then.)

Because of something that has nothing to do with the movie? (Maybe, but what?)

I finally figured it out that night as I was drifting off to sleep. The thing that had been BUGGING me ever since I'd found out about Joe's role in the movie.

Joe was going on an adventure without me. He was leaving me behind.

Things would **never be the same** again.

I GNORED

Over the next five days at school, Bec and Joe didn't talk to me. I understood, because **I deserved it** after how I'd acted at lunch.

Every morning, everyone FOUGHT to sit next to Joe. And every day, I sat next to James Goh. If **Ms. Stacey** noticed what was going on, she didn't mention it to me.

I bought my new bike after school on Monday. On Tuesday, I rode it to school.

It wasn't as EXCITING to ride as I thought it would be. Half of the fun of the bike had been planning for it with Joe. We'd looked at bike catalogs for months.

Now that I finally had my new bike, **I wanted to share it with him.** But I knew for sure that wasn't going to happen.

It seemed like the whole school had gone *Two Stone County* crazy.

The principal called a meeting on Tuesday afternoon to announce that the producers of the show had chosen our school to be in the film.

Our school building was really old, over 100 years old. **Some of the food in the cafeteria was almost that old, too.**

"Because of this honor," said **Principal Woods**, "the whole school will be on cleaning duty all day on Thursday."

A groan ran around the room.

Principal Woods went on, "Let's show Hollywood what Bays Park is made of!"

Someone at the front of the room cheered, but the rest of us GROANED again and went back to our classrooms.

On Wednesday morning, Rose came by my desk. She wanted to let me know that she had a part in the movie.

I congratulated her. That took the smile off her face, and she went back to her own desk.

A couple of other kids from my class had been to auditions too. They kept talking about it until Ms. Stacey made us take a **vow of silence** for one whole hour.

Usually an hour of quiet time would kill me, but I wasn't very interested in talking to anyone. Except Joe, who was pretending I was 𝕀ℕ𝕍𝕀𝕊𝕀𝔹𝕃𝔼.

It turned out that our school wasn't the only place to get into the Hollywood spirit.

Our town's daily newspaper, *The Bays Park Times*, was always putting something about the movie on  the front page. There were usually **glamorous** photos of stars. The gossip column was running **rumors** about who might be starring in the movie. The want ads had large advertisements asking for antique furniture, farm equipment, and clothing.

The mayor of Bays Park, who loved getting his picture in the paper, kept being quoted in the paper. He said, **"This movie is putting Bays Park on the map!"** I thought that was kind of strange, because I've seen maps of our state, and Bays Park was 𝔻𝔼𝔽𝕀ℕ𝕀𝕋𝔼𝕃𝕐 already there.

In another article in the paper, the police commissioner talked about possible road closures while the movie was filming. There was also a story about a psychic who predicted **a hurricane** coming to town. She said it would wipe out everything — the movie's cast and crew.

The whole town was **different**. Stores that I'd known all my life suddenly changed overnight.

The Chunky Chicken restaurant became Ye Olde Chicken Shoppe. They sold Two Stone County chicken packs and Wild West Cola, which was just their regular cola but with a different name.

Sampson's Drugstore became Sampson's Feed and Grain Store, even though the only grain they were selling was the **wholegrain bread** in their bakery section. The gas station became Bays Park Saddlery. My favorite candy store changed its name to Two Stone County's Sweets Store.

It was enough to make you think Bays Park was **stuck in a time warp.**

Rose Thornton's mom said that we should rename the town square Two Stone County Town Square.

I saw her talking about it on TV, and when 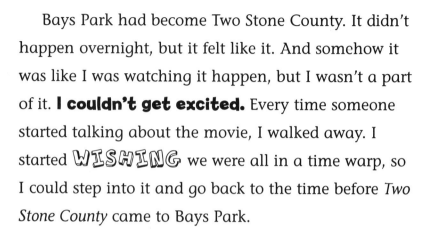 I looked really closely, I could see Rose in the background casually walking past **about ten times.**

Bays Park had become Two Stone County. It didn't happen overnight, but it felt like it. And somehow it was like I was watching it happen, but I wasn't a part of it. **I couldn't get excited.** Every time someone started talking about the movie, I walked away. I started 𝕎𝕀𝕊𝕳𝕀ℕ𝔾 we were all in a time warp, so I could step into it and go back to the time before *Two Stone County* came to Bays Park.

I tried to talk to Dad about it. All he said was, "That movie has pulled this town together. I've never seen such a **spirit of cooperation** here before."

I tried talking to Zoe about it.

"Dribbles, let's face it," she said. *"You're just jealous."*

I felt like she'd hit me with a brick. Make that **two bricks.**

I pointed to my chest. "Me? Jealous?" I said.

Zoe nodded.

"Jealous of what? **You're crazy.** You don't know what you're saying," I said. My voice was getting higher and higher.

"You're usually the star," Zoe said. "*The one in the spotlight.* You're jealous. And you can't deal with the fact that Joe did something without you telling him what to think and what to do."

"I don't tell Joe what to do!" I said. My voice was so high that it was squeaking.

"Whatever you say," Zoe said. "Joe has moved to a new phase in his life. Maybe you should **deal with it.**"
Luckily, she went back to her room then, before my voice completely disappeared into the clouds.

"Me? Tell Joe what to do?" I muttered. "Whatever."

Boris waddled by, so I gave him a scratch behind the ear.

"Have you ever heard anything so 𝕊𝕋𝕌ℙ𝕀𝔻?" I asked him.

Boris just looked at me and kept walking.

Then I called **Bec**.

Before she could hang up, I asked quickly, "Do you think I'm *Jealous* of Joe?"

"Yep," said Bec.

"Do you need to think about that?" I asked.

"**No,**" she said. Then she hung up.

I had my answer.

Now I just had to deal with it.

CHAPTER 11

THE PLAN

I wanted to call Joe right away to tell him that I knew what a jerk I'd been. But I didn't think it would help. I could talk until the *Two Stone County* cows came home, but that didn't mean Joe would believe me.

No. I needed to show Joe that I meant what I said. So I decided to have a surprise party. The party would be so **amazingly good** that Joe would have to forgive me. **That seemed easy enough.**

Plan A — talk to Mom.

"Mom," I said, "I want to have a surprise party at our house."

"No," she said.

"Why?" I asked.

"It's not your birthday," said **Mom**.

"It's not for my birthday," I told her. Then I explained.

Mom still shook her head. "It's a nice idea," she said, "but we just repainted the house. The thought of fingerprints on my fresh walls is TERRIBLE. So, no."

That was the end of Plan A. So I went to Plan B.

"**Dad**," I said, "I want to have a surprise party at our house."

"What did your mother say?" he asked.

So I tried Plan C. I wasn't looking forward to Plan C. It involved talking to Gran.

I waited until she came over for lunch. I ran out to help her. This time there were three **huge spiky plants** in the back seat of her car. One of the plants poked me in the eye when I bent over to pick it up.

"What took you so long?" Gran asked when I picked up the plants.

"Hi, Gran," I said. "Your car looks very, um, shiny today." **Gran loved her car.**

"I know," she said. "I'm using a new car wash. Makes all the difference."

She spent the next hour talking about the difference between car wash A and car wash B and whether you could **wax your car** too much and whether leather seats were better than fabric-covered seats.

The whole time, I nodded and helped her into her **FAVORITE** chair and got her some iced tea and brought the rest of the things in from her car.

Finally, I was getting sick of nodding. Gran slurped her iced tea and said, "So what do you want?"

"Want?" I echoed.

"David, I *wasn't born yesterday*," she said. Then she chuckled. "Or the day before."

"Or the day before that!" I added with a laugh.

Gran stopped smiling.

"Well, **I have a plan** and I want you to help me," I said.

So I told Gran all about the surprise party. I told her how I wanted it to be a CELEBRATION for everyone who was involved in the *Two Stone County* movie, **especially the locals.**

And I told her how I wanted to make it up to Joe, because I'd been acting like his **worst enemy**, not his **real friend.**

Gran nodded every now and then but let me talk. Finally, she asked, "So, what did your mother say when you asked her?"

I told her. Gran nodded again.

"I think a surprise party is a **good idea**," she said. "I need to think about it. Can you let me do that, David?"

I could have hugged her. In fact, I did. **She almost hit me with her walking stick.**

"Now, what's that smell?" she asked. "Is your mother BURNING lunch?"

* * *

Gran is the chairperson of the Historical Society. I already mentioned that. So when she got on the phone that afternoon, she talked the whole Historical Society into having the surprise party at the Bays Park Historical Hall.

"So you've got somewhere to have the ₱Ⱥℝ₸Ɏ," she told me. "Now what?"

I knew what my next move should be. "An ad in the paper," I said.

I wanted to put an ad in *The Bay Park Times*. It would invite every local person involved in *Two Stone County* to come to a **special meeting** next Saturday. Then, at the meeting, we would Ṩ𝕌ℝ₱ℝℐṨℰ them with a party.

"Who's going to *pay* for the food and decorations?" asked **Gran**.

I'd already thought of that.

I'd only ridden my new bike once, and that was to school the morning after I'd bought it.

So I talked to the guy at the bike store. He agreed to buy it back, at a **discounted price**, of course. With the money I got for the bike, I would be able to buy **TONS** of snacks and still have money left to decorate the hall.

When I told Gran, she frowned. "Are you sure you want to do that?" she asked me quietly.

"Definitely," I said.

Gran knew someone at the *The Bays Park Times*, so she got the ad for me.

Once the ad was in the paper, **everyone** in town was talking about it. Lots of people were coming to the party. I hoped they wouldn't be too **thirsty**.

"They can always drink water," said Mom. "Now, how many lasagnas do you want me to make?"

If anyone at home noticed that my bike was missing, they didn't mention it.

At school, I sat next to James Goh. **Rose** was *bragging* about her part in the movie, what makeup she'd be wearing, and what color looked best on her, and how **FAMOUS** she was going to be.

Joe must have gotten sick of having a new desk buddy every day, because Bec spent the week sitting next to him. A couple of times, I wanted to say hi, but Bec had such a **big frown** on her face that I kept on walking.

I stayed away from our usual tree at lunch. I wondered if they were having Secret Club meetings **without me.**

When Saturday finally came, time sped up like it was on **fast forward.**

It seemed like one minute I woke up early. The next minute, I was GOBBLING down breakfast. The next minute, I was decorating the Historical Hall with **Zoe** and **Harry**. The next minute, people were arriving at the door.

The official meeting time was one o'clock. Bec and Joe arrived on time, but I waited until 1:15 to make sure everyone was there. Then I went to the microphone on stage.

Gran stood off to one side of the stage, leaning on her walking stick. I wondered if she was worried that I would **break** something. On the other side of the stage, Zoe was waiting for my instructions.

"**Testing. Testing**," I said, tapping the microphone. "Thank you, everyone, for coming today."

"**Where are the cameras?**" someone yelled from the back of the room.

"Where's Harrison Ford?" someone else yelled. It sounded like Mr. Edwards, our school janitor.

Gran marched out to the microphone and pushed me aside. "*Would all of you please be quiet?*" she yelled.

The room fell silent. Then Gran handed the microphone back to me.

"Like I was saying, thank you for coming today," I said. "You're probably wondering what this meeting is about. I just thought someone needed to say what a GREAT JOB everyone's doing, pulling together to make this movie. Soon the whole world's going to know, Bays Park is the best!"

I nodded at Zoe. She nodded back and pulled on a rope. Then the curtain behind me opened to show a handmade glittery sign that read **"Congratulations Bays Park and Joe Pagnopolous!"**

The "OUS" on Pagnopolous was a little squished because we almost ran out of room on the sign.

I nodded at Zoe again. Two hundred balloons should have fallen down from the ceiling then, but **only about three fell down.** Then Mom and Dad began bringing out the food and drinks and people clapped.

The place was **buzzing**. I hopped off the stage and went to find Joe and Bec. I finally found them in the kitchen helping out with the food.

"Hey, Joe," I said.

"Hey," said Joe. "David, this is AMAZING. You didn't have to. Thank you. Thanks so much."

"I'm really sorry," I said.

"It's okay, David, really," said **Joe**.

The crowd got quiet again. Rose Thornton's mom was onstage. She was holding a sheet of paper.

"I am sorry to *rain on everyone's parade*," **Mrs. Thornton** said. "But I have some bad news."

She was quiet for a second. Then she took a deep breath and said, "The producers of *Two Stone County* have just canceled the production."

"What? What did she say?" someone yelled.

"There's not going to be a movie," said Mrs. Thornton.

An ANGRY murmur ran through the crowd. People started yelling.

"They can't do this to us!"

"*But what about my acting career?*"

"I changed my store's sign. Who's going to pay me back?"

Suddenly, Gran grabbed the microphone again.

"Quiet!" she boomed. She waited for the noise to die down. "What sort of manners are these, ladies and gentlemen?" **Gran** asked. "This young man here, my grandson, David Mortimore Baxter, has thrown a party in your honor. In honor of your hard work and cooperation. It seems to me that none of that's changed. And that's something to be PROUD of."

She took a deep breath. Then she finished by saying, "So let's forget about *Two Stone County*. Let's celebrate being part of Bays Park!"

Then Zoe jumped onstage. She turned on some music and yelled, **"Let's party!"**

Joe didn't seem too worried about missing out on his shot at Hollywood. It turned out that his part in the movie was "Walking Boy 3." All he had to do was walk past the camera in the last scene.

"So you didn't even have to talk?" I asked.

Joe shook his head. "Nope. Also, Rose was 'Walking Girl 4,'" he told us.

Bec and Joe laughed. I grabbed a
soda bottle and started to talk into it
like a 𝕄𝕀ℂℝ𝕆ℙℍ𝕆ℕ𝔼.

"I'd like to thank my agent," I said. "My producer
and director. My co-stars. The walking-by cast — you
all do an amazing job, really, guys. And, of course,
my friends, Bec and Joe. **I couldn't have done it
without you. You two rock!**"

About the Author

When Karen Tayleur was growing up, her father told her many stories about his own childhood. These stories continued to grow. She says, "I always enjoyed the retelling, and wanted to create a character who had the same abilities with 'bending the truth.'" And David Mortimore Baxter was born! Karen lives in Australia with her husband, two children, two cats, and one dog.

About the Illustrator

Brann Garvey lives in Minneapolis, Minnesota, with his wife, Keegan, their dog, Lola, and their very fat cat, Iggy. Brann graduated from Iowa State University with a bachelor of fine arts degree. He later attended the Minneapolis College of Art and Design, where he studied illustration. In his free time, Brann enjoys being with his family and friends. He brings his sketchbook everywhere he goes.

Glossary

amateur (AM-uh-chur)—someone who is new to a business

announcement (uh-NOUNSS-muhnt)—a speech made publicly or officially

audition (aw-DISH-uhn)—a short performance by an actor to see whether he or she is suitable for a part

autograph (AW-tuh-graf)—a person's signature

cast (KAST)—the actors in a play or movie

crew (KROO)—a team of people who work together to make a movie

director (duh-REK-tur)—the main person in charge of making a movie

extras (EK-struhz)—actors in a movie who have very small roles

focus (FOH-kuhss)—attention

local (LOH-kuhl)—if something is local, it comes from the area where you live

pioneers (pye-uh-NEERZ)—people who explored unknown territory and settled there

private (PRYE-vit)—belonging to one person

producer (pruh-DOOSS-ur)—a person in charge of making a movie

role (ROHL)—the part a person acts in a movie

Discussion Questions

1. Why was David mean to Joe during their Sunday lunch?

2. If a movie was filmed in your town, what are some of the things that would change? Do you think it would be fun or not? Talk about your answers.

3. As a group, cast your own movie. Who would be the star? Who would be the extras? Who would direct the movie? Who would work behind the scenes, choosing costumes, doing makeup, or filming the movie? Don't forget to give your movie a name!

Writing Prompts

1. Write about a time you were jealous of a friend. Why were you jealous? How did you resolve the problem?

2. What's your favorite movie? Choose a character from that movie and write about them. What would it be like to be that character for a day?

3. Try writing chapter 11 from Joe's point of view. How does he feel? What does he see and hear? Write about it!

DAVID MORTIMORE BAXTER

David is a great kid, but he has one big problem — he can't stop talking. These wildly humorous stories, told by David himself, will show readers just how much trouble a boy and his mouth can get into, whether he's going on a class trip, trying to find a missing neighbor, running a detective agency, or getting lost in the wild. David is amiable, engaging, cool, and smart enough to realize that growing up is the biggest adventure of all.

With David!

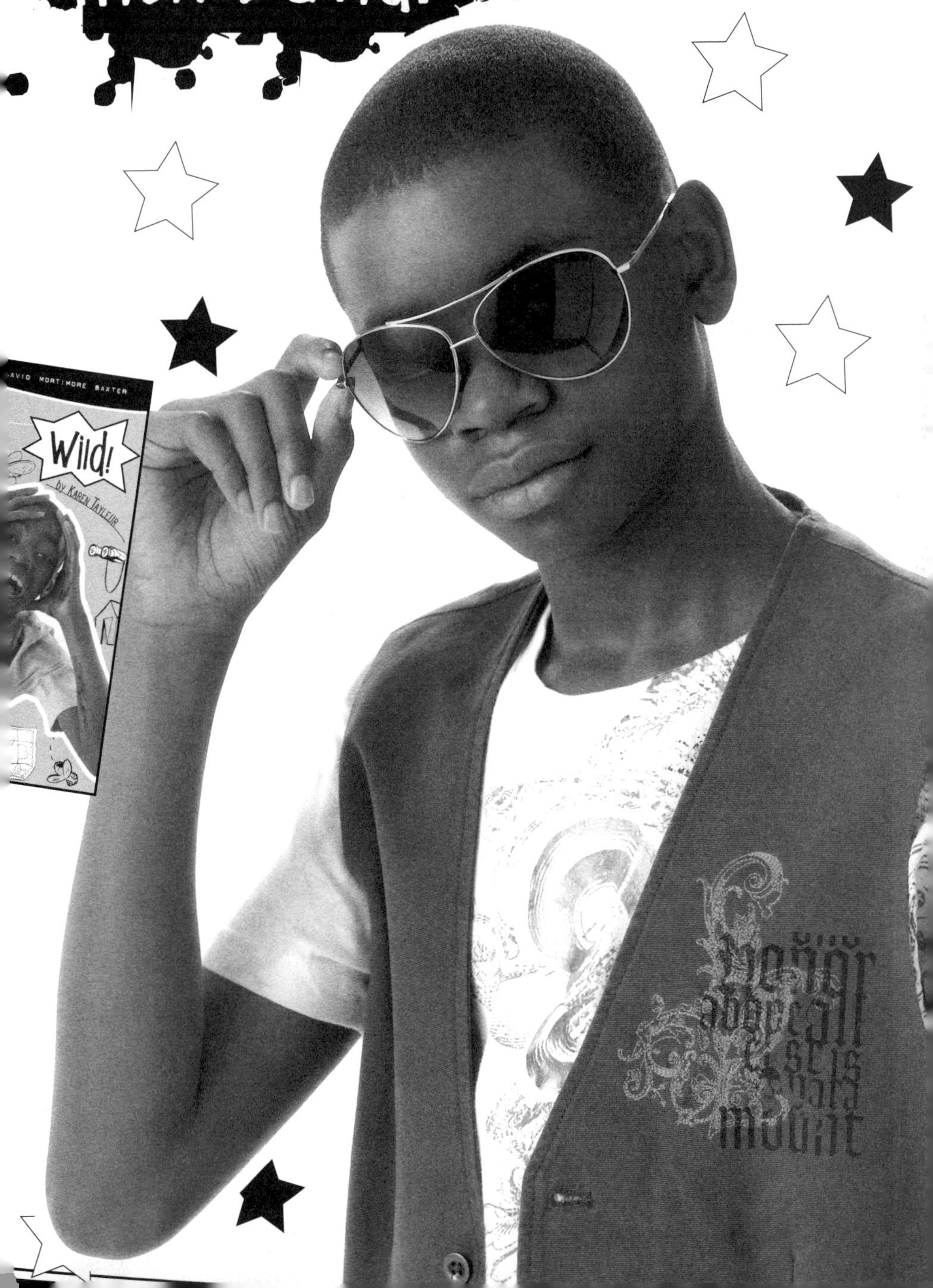

Internet Sites

Do you want to know more about subjects related to this book? Or are you interested in learning about other topics? Then check out FactHound, a fun, easy way to find Internet sites.

Our investigative staff has already sniffed out great sites for you!

Here's how to use FactHound:

1. Visit *www.facthound.com*

2. Select your grade level.

3. To learn more about subjects related to this book, type in the book's ISBN number: 9781434211989.

4. Click the **Fetch It** button.

FactHound will fetch the best Internet sites for you!